MID-TWENTIES SYNDROME

Connor Thompson

authorHOUSE®

AuthorHouse™ UK
1663 Liberty Drive
Bloomington, IN 47403 USA
www.authorhouse.co.uk
Phone: 0800.197.4150

This is a work of fiction. All of the characters, names, incidents, organizations, and dialogue in
this novel are either the products of the author's imagination or are used fictitiously.

Published by AuthorHouse 08/24/2016

ISBN: 978-1-5246-3777-4 (sc)
ISBN: 978-1-5246-3776-7 (e)

Print information available on the last page.

Dedication

For Alice, who always showed enthusiasm about my aspirations.

Contents

Foreword
by Niall Baxter

With little to no knowledge of what the fuck this book consists of, I was asked to write a foreword for it by Mr Connor Thompson. Over the last few months I have ignored his requests to read over his short stories due to the fact I couldn't give a shit about them. I feel confident in writing this here as Connor is stupid enough to think that I am just being ironic. Stupid enough to think I'm just jabbing him. I'm not. Why am I not? Because I benefit absolutely nothing from the publishing (*or self-publishing, way to go Connor, no publisher would read your drivel*) of his book. I have my own shit to deal with. My own shit consisting of the fact I haven't washed my bedsheets for over a month. Is that jizz? Probably. I have University deadlines looming over me right fucking now. Literally as I write this foreword I have a deadline that I have already gone over, but intend to submit tomorrow due to the fact I know my lecturer won't be checking his pigeon-hole over the weekend. And being the true master-procrastinator that I am, I've opted to write this pillock's foreword instead of cracking on with my reflective essay (*which shouldn't even be a thing*) in which I'll talk absolute bollocks about how Shakespeare has influenced my stage-play about inept gangsters fucking each other over in a basement. And yes, it's better than anything you'll read in this book. Except for this foreword of course.

I would insist on a cut of the profits for writing this if I wasn't so confident in the fact no one would be idiotic enough to buy it.

For all you know Connor could have written (*wrote? (who gives a fuck?)*) this foreword himself and claimed it was his friend Niall Baxter that did it. Bullshit. Connor doesn't have any friends. Why do you think he spends his time writing short stories? I apologise to Connor's family that may end up reading this. I'm being horrible about your son/brother/uncle/nephew/cousin/grandson but the fact of the matter is, still, that I don't give a toss.

I've lived with this half-Geordie, zebra-print boxer wearing, Auschwitz mistaking (*that's an inside joke, he once drunkenly thought that Auschwitz was a person*) sad act for over three years now and for some fucked up reason, probably the fact that I'm as much a gimp as he is, plan on living with him again. The fucked up reason? I look at Connor and I feel infinitely better about myself. When he doesn't wear socks I feel disgust, but then I remember that I'm not so depraved to do something so inhumane. And that is the reason you should just read this fucking book. It'll be over soon. Like sitting through an episode of Jeremy Kyle. It'll be mind-numbingly shit, but when you've eventually finished it you will feel spectacular compared to what you have just witnessed. Because if this insufferable cunt can write a book (*albeit self-published and a series of short stories because he is incapable of keeping his mind on something for over an hour*) there's an endless abyss of possibilities as to what you can achieve. Whether it be managing an extra few sit-ups at the gym, speeding up a few paces to catch the bus to your shit job, squeezing in your nineteenth wank of a bank holiday or getting that extra inch of your dildo into your gaping, demolished arsehole... Just remember one thing:

Connor Thompson wrote a fucking (self-published) *book.*

Acknowledgments

Thank you to Mammy and Daddy for paying for this to happen. I suddenly felt pressure when it became real; I was like 'shit, this had better be good.' Because if it's not, would they be angry and say: 'We've just spunked £500 at the wall for this shite, you're grounded,' or 'Connor, I divin't kna where yi got this shite from,' no, of course not. I'm sure they'd be proud that I've attempted something like this. Thank you anyways. Also, thanks Dad, for the time you sent us a care package full of frozen food (including broth) which resulted in myself and wor Kyle standing in the post office as the man gave us a big bag containing a leaking box. It stank of curry. Thank you to everyone I sent these stories to and hounded for feedback, you know who you are. Not that you helped at all, you're all absolutely useless and I only did it to make you feel important. Thanks to everyone else who helped me with reading it and whatnot; you know who you are. Thank you to Ashington and Preston for being places which helped manifest many rants that appear in this book. Thanks to Daniella for the front cover. Thanks to Bill McCoid for setting up a module where this became possible. Also, thanks for taking us to Carnforth that day, as that manifested into loads of absolute tosh which you're about to read. Thanks to Joel for being cool.

Introduction

Who is Connor Thompson and why should I read his book? Fuck knows but you are. As I write this, I'm currently doing a Masters in Scriptwriting at UCLan in Preston and this book is essentially coursework. It's not just boring assignment criteria that I'm trying to match, I chose to write a book of short stories for a project. Why? I don't know; something different. Funny thing is that we're not actually marked on the content we create but how we go about getting something released or made. So I've basically just flooded this book with short stories about anything I fucking want. Some are stories where I wander into a chasm of bullshit, some are observations that branch off life experiences and things that have pissed me off and others are just rants. But aye, it's mainly just shite.

It's not as half-arsed as it sounds though; I spent about eight months writing these stories. Many of the stories are based on real things; the story about a bus driver is to accentuate my hatred for some bus drivers and the story about the Australian lass going to Carnforth is based on my visit to Carnforth and finding out the clock was a lie. Not really a lie but someone said it wasn't the complete same as in the film. I mainly write scripts. so short stories are very different for me but I think I did my best. Christ, I better pack this in now before it starts to sound like an evaluation essay. Anyways, I have no idea if I'll keep this up. We'll just see how this goes. I hope you enjoy it, if you don't then I'll get my dad to knack your dad.

The Pool Trick-Shot Montage

This bus driver though. I got him good. Nothing brutal or violent or anything, but I got him good. Don't you *dare* roll your eyes at me when I present a ten pound note when it's three pound thirty; that's an acceptable transaction, so why are you being a stroppy little wanker? Oh aye, because you've got to go through the inconvenience of rustling through your pocket for a five pound note instead of giving me six pound coins. What's wrong with giving me six pound coins? Don't you *dare* piss me off.

This has baffled me since I started getting buses and I've always had a sort of rivalry with every single bus driver I came across, particularly the ones in Northumberland (my roots). This one guy wouldn't let me on because I was five pence short - I was fourteen as well. I happen to think that was the same bus driver who wouldn't let my Grandma on because her pension pass was out of date by a few days, leaving her no choice but to walk a mile where not even a walking stick could prevent her struggle; she was 64 at this time. She complained to the powers that be and I haven't seen him operate a bus since. Good riddance you Buzz Lightyear-looking cunt.

But aye, the guy who rolled his wanky eyes at me. That was the first time I had taken a bus at home for ages and an opportunity arose that I had to take. I'm a freelance filmmaker and I have my details on local websites advertising what I can do. It's not my full time job, just a hobby and a way to make a quick buck. A few days after the incident, I checked to see if I had any enquiries. There were a few boring ones like weddings – I hate doing weddings, a local advert for a painter, who was also a window cleaner and a pool trick shot montage. This person wanted jump cuts of his skills on a pool table, to put himself on the map. I'm not sure who would be interested though. 'For sports bars and Universities' he wrote in the description. You wouldn't guess who put that enquiry through. You wouldn't *believe* who wanted a montage of his skills on a pool table...

Aye. A bus driver. Not the Buzz Lightyear one, I wouldn't give him the time of fucking day. It was the spiffy little minge who hates giving change. He mustn't have recognized me on my picture! I thought it might be a laugh so I arranged to meet him at a pub, plus I'd maybe have a little confrontation with him, seeing as through he annoyed me. I took all of the equipment I had; cameras, lights and tripods. I got there and he still hadn't recognised me. He shook my hand and said 'it's a pleasure.' Very formal for a bus driver, is it not? Anyways, he was keen to get started.

So I set everything up, tripods for multi-camera angels, I don't mess about – this is going to be class. He was really excited. I just told him to go for it. 'Pull of as many different shots as you can, take your time and don't worry if you mess it up. I can edit it out so it's just the good ones.' He was giddy, he did a few crackers then messed up a few times. 'Don't worry about it mate, it never happened,' I said with a cheeky wink.

It was fortunate that I had brought hefty memory cards for my cameras cause the cunt went on for hours. Mind you, some of his shots were amazing, some were shite though. He finally threw down the pool cue, covered in sweat. He looked like a lumberjack that had just finished hacking the utter fuck out of a tree. That was it. He was so proud of himself. 'Right, well done. I'll edit this together then get it straight back to you.' He asked if I could get it done by the weekend as he was having his 50th birthday party with all of his family and friends and would like to show off the film. 'Oh aye mate, it'll be ready by then. Don't you worry.'

I didn't sleep that night, or the night after. I wanted to get the film right for him. Every shot mattered, every frame had to be the correct length and corresponded with the previous shot – even though it was a montage. Not a wink of sleep; I was on cheap energy drink. Guzzling pure petrol just to keep going. I even disconnected the internet to avoid distraction. It worked. I had finished. My Casanova was complete. I hit export and burnt it to a DVD. I waltzed along to the party, which he had graciously invited me to. I got there, his whole family were excited to see it; it seemed that he had been building them up to it all week. On the contrary for him, he was anxious as hell. 'Did you get it right?' he asked frequently. I kept assuring him it was fine as I put the disc in the computer which was set up to a projector. I looked at him 'it's time.' He got the attention of his people and said 'here it is,' to which they responded by a vigorous, excitable murmur. I hit play and sat down at the back of the room.

Miss, miss, miss, miss, miss, miss. Not a single trick shot. All of the blunders. I edited together all of the shite shots. The audience were howling. He looks over to me, a tear rolls down his cheek. 'Why?' he mouths. I nod towards the screen. The final shot where he splits and falls over gets a ruckus of laughter then a black screen with the words. 'There's nothing wrong with change.' Aye, he understood. I got him good.

The Best Mugger in Ashington

Kiefer Cairns was the best mugger in Ashington. Everybody knew who he was, some through friendship, some through trepidation. He was infamous for his mugging skills. So skillful that it wouldn't be inaccurate to say you'd be somewhat honoured to be mugged from Kiefer Cairns. It'd be like 'Ah, fuck. I've been mugged.' Sob sob sob and all that. Then you'd be like 'Er wey, I got mugged off of Kiefer Cairns. Fair play.' You'd skill be miffed that you lost your wallet or watch or whatever, but you'd wonder when it happened. Kiefer Cairns was so skilled that you wouldn't even know *when* you were mugged. He's a pure shadow.

It was a strange situation; people would even greet him on the street. They'd jokingly ask him 'mugging anyone special today?' to which Kiefer Cairns would reply 'oh, maybe! Might be your dad, hehe,' with a mischievous smile. It was his age-old technique that made him so popular; a technique that nobody knew the details of. This was then. Before the incident. The incident that muggers would talk about for years and years and years and years. But now, all has been revealed. People started to talk. The secret has been released – like a Jackdaw that's been stuck in the loft being let out into the wild.

His technique was simply called 'woah, sorry mate'. That's it. It's all about the moment in which he'd say these words to someone after 'accidentally' walking into someone, because see, for Kiefer Cairns, he had the power to stretch a moment to as long as he wanted. Weeks, months, even years. Well, not really, but he had cracking reflexes. So, take this example. Folk have long been referring to the classic case of when he mugged Callum Whinfield's iPod Nano.

It was a birthday present. Something Callum Whinfield really wanted for so long. He finally got it for his 14th birthday. He'd flash it around the school playground like he thinks he's the tits but everyone's had a Nano for weeks; he was late to the party and everyone knew it – 'We don't care that you've got an iPod Nano, Callum, especially when you're always listening to *Simple Plan*.' He was one of them people in your class that wasn't very popular because he took Violin lessons. When he got mugged, not a lot of people had any sympathy for him when he did get mugged. He was walking home from Violin practice with his Nano headphones plugged securely in. He walks into a strange man; 'woah, sorry mate,' the man said. 'No problem at all,' replies Callum Whinfield, who walks into the evening without a worry in the world. That was until the next day, though. 'Mum, where's my iPod?' –

Let's just hold on a second here, let's pause the story. I wrote 'Mum' up there on purpose. I say 'Mam.' Nearly everyone says 'Mam' where I'm from, but I've been living in Lancashire for the last four years and everyone says 'Mum' here, so it's refreshing to go back up home and hear it said correctly. Saying that, there were some people up home who would say 'Mum' which annoys the fuck out of me. Basically, if you said 'Mum' instead of 'Mam' and you lived in Ashington, you were a bad person. Not really, I don't mean that. But I do. Anyways, back to the story-

'Mum, where's my iPod Nano?' asks Callum Whinfield. She's got no idea. 'You didn't have it when you came in last night,' she says. He clicks on. He replays the incident with the strange man. 'Woah, sorry mate.' Time slows down. The strange man nips into Callum Whinfield's pocket and takes out the iPod Nano and whips it into his own pocket. Fury sores through his veins. He's not 'feeling honoured' or anything, he has no respect for Kiefer Cairns. He wants revenge.

He was just one of the many, many preys of Kiefer Cairns. He didn't even really need the items that he took; he would treasure them as trophies, just look at his cabinet. Flooded with goodies, a PlayStation memory card, countless watches, phones, walkmans and sure enough, Callum Whinfield's iPod Nano. He had mugged nearly everyone in Ashington, or had he? There was someone who Kiefer Cairns couldn't ever mug, no matter how hard he tried, someone new on the mugging scene. Someone even better than Kiefer Cairns. Someone Kiefer Cairns just could not mug to save his life; he had attempted to set traps and even follow this person. He was a shadow and nobody knew who he was. For Kiefer Cairns though, the most frustrating thing about this person was that he was a mugger as well. This mugger *had* mugged most of the people in the town, so stealthy that nobody even knew he existed. He was so stealthy that people would assume that Kiefer Cairns did the muggings. But he didn't. Kiefer Cairns was a fraud. He would hate himself for it, but took the credit nonetheless. The only way Kiefer Cairns could rectify his place in society is if he put an end to this episode and mugged this mysterious enigma.

But Kiefer Cairns had come into some intel. Some *reliable* intel. Intel that Kiefer Cairns trusted. The itinerary of the stranger. A time and place. 7pm at the bridge outside Wilkinsons. Word was that he was going to graffiti some distasteful words on the pass. But Kiefer Cairns wasn't worried about that. He would finally get him. Kiefer Cairns sat and waited, watching the tick by on a watch he mugged. It strikes six o'clock. Time to get ready. He throws on his trusty mugging jacket (a green kagoul) and sets off.

He takes hide in a nearby alcove. He waits and counts the seconds. This could define him as a mugger. This is the big one. This is a diamond shop heist. This is Apollo fourteen, or whatever number we're on now. He hears movement, he peaks – it's him. His hood is up; his face is hidden behind a shadow. He is dressed fully in black, he stops in his tracks, silent in his approach, he looks around and takes out a spray can and sprays something on the wall. Kiefer Cairns takes a deep breath, this is it. He stands up and walks towards him.

What the mustard!? He's gone. All that remains is a discarded spray can. Kiefer Cairns can't believe it. He picks up the spray can and throws it against the wall. On the wall reads 'R.I.P. Kiefer Cairns lmfao,' underneath it is a small drawing of a guitar, or was it a violin? Could it be!? Kiefer Cairns screams to the heavens.

The ball is back in Kiefer Cairns' court. What must he do!? He takes Callum Whinfield's iPod Nano and plugs it into iTunes. He clicks on 'forgot your password?', thinking it'd supply e-mail address. Bugger! He unplugs it in a strop but then... hold on a minute. If he *had* mugged Callum Whinfield, who indeed is the stranger, does that mean he has defeated him before? Or maybe the stranger is dropping hints to make Kiefer Cairns *think* that Callum Whinfield is the stranger and is *expecting* Kiefer Cairns to visit Callum Whinfield's house to get answers. A-ha! Kiefer Cairns has an opportunity here. If only he knew Callum Whinfield's address. He picks up the Nano and flips it. Oh yes. The classic 'if found, return to so and so,' on the back. Too easy? Of course it was, the stranger *wanted* Kiefer Cairns to find it.

Let the planning begin! Kiefer Cairns begins by buying two green kagouls and hiring two associates to pose as Kiefer Cairns. The first Kiefer Cairns impersonator walked up to the house and knocked on the door. The second Kiefer Cairns impersonator 'snuck' around the back to the tree house. The real Kiefer Cairns was in the house opposite, observing through binoculars. He waited, keeping a firm eye on the second impersonator. Sure enough, it worked. The stranger stood under the treehouse, waiting for the second impersonator to give away his position. Time for the real Kiefer Cairns to make his move.

The stranger lurks under the tree house, he hears movement from above. The second Kiefer Cairns impersonator leaps out of the tree house. 'Nice try,' whispers the stranger, to which the second Kiefer Cairns impersonator turns around. He's been done. The stranger stutters as the impersonator runs away in fear. The stranger turns around and there, Dean Cairns stands. The stranger stood aghast, Dean Cairns shoves the stranger – 'woah, sorry mate,' he says sarcastically. And he mugs him.

And it was a big mug. He had been leading up to this mug his whole life. He put so much strain and effort into this mug. So much sweat and endeavor went into this mug. So much elbow grease went into this mug that Kiefer Cairns, not only stole every item on the stranger's person, not only stole every bit of clothing on his body but he stole his entire identity. Kiefer Cairns became the stranger! Mortified, yet gleeful about his victory, he was now able to find out who the mysterious stranger was. He could finally look upon his nemesis who has been kicking him down over the years and openingly mocking his efforts. The time had come. Was it Callum Whinfield?

No. It was Antony Worrall Thompson.

As for Callum Whinfield, I don't know, he was too much of a wuss to plot his revenge, probably crying in his *Mum's* arms.

T-shirts

I used to want to collect as many cool t-shirts as possible but now I feel embarrassed by most of the ones I own. Mainly because of how outdated they are to me. There will be times where I have accidentally been forced into a conversation with a stranger about my Batman t-shirt. I don't like talking to those strangers because I don't know where to look. I hate eye contact with people, I'm better with it now but with a geek in a game shop, I hate it. From now on, all my t-shirts will be of patterns of colours. It's not even that I don't like Batman or the things on my t-shirts, I just don't like having them.

Also, I don't want that t-shirt to represent me as a person. I am paranoid about people looking at my t-shirt and think 'well, he's wearing *that* t-shirt so he's *this* kind of person.' I want my clothes to provoke as little interaction as possible. However, if it's just a nice shirt, like a nice pattern or whatever then that's OK. But I just don't want people to see that I once collected three empty packets of Monster Munch and paid a fiver just to get a Monster Munch t-shirt. I don't want people to see that.

I wrote in my Excel document for this book that I would stretch this to 500 words but I feel that I've quickly summarized how much of a miserable bastard so I'll just write what I'm doing right now as I write this.

I'm on a train sitting opposite a man who is reading a book really fast. From what I can see, the text is quite small, but fuck me, he's reading it as fast as Nobby Solano used to read the game. This man is married, wearing a Nike t-shirt and eating coconut pretzels. I mean, that's interesting to me. I wonder what his story is. I might ask him, 'here mate, what's going on?'. He looks friendly but I don't think he looks friendly enough to reply to something like that. I don't know what that means; I don't know how someone can look frie- oh my god he just got a phone call. That was quick. Anyways, what if he's a really important scientist or something? I just realized that he's got headphones coming out of his Nike t-shirt but they're not in his ears. How extraordinary. This man could be my dad. I mean, I've already got a dad but what if I was adopted and this coconut pretzel eating warlock is my pop. Daddy? He looks quite sporty because he's got a sporty-looking bag, probably stuffed to the brim with sporty things. Like shoes. He's been on the same page of his book for a while now...Holy shit...what if he's *pretending* to read and is thinking the same thing as me!? 'Is that my son?' – Oh my god, he's put the book down. The book is down. He's on his phone now, typing. What is he's writing 'on the train and saw my son. K bye.' – He just got up and went somewhere. Oh he got off at Penrith. Bye Daddy.

'The Checkout'

The supermarket was strangely packed for a Tuesday evening. Lines of people attached to the three out of six checkouts that were operating. All I wanted was my tin of ravioli. Thirty-seven pence. I was crammed between other customers with large baskets of items that would take ages to pay for (it was one of those discounted supermarkets where you had to bring your own bags and stuff your items in yourself, unless you buy your own bags.) Movement between shoppers was very few and far between, as was the conveyer belt with the items; it was a very jerky stop-start situation every time it moved, and when it did there was a rather horrible 'clunk-clunk...clunk' sound from a single bottle of wine wedged in between two of those 'next customer please' triangle things. It was sounds that made me infuriatingly twitch at the idea that someone would do that. To lie the fucking bottle down so it rolls every time the belt moves. 'Who would do such a thing?' I thought, 'what kind of human being wouldn't just stand the bottle up?' It made me sick. Why didn't they stand it up? 'God, why?' I demanded the gods for an answer. Maybe whoever put it there figured that it would fall down if it was standing up, well if that's the case – why have it on the conveyer belt to begin with? It's one fucking item.

Some time had passed, it perhaps wouldn't have if the till operator showed any signs of being skilled in his work. All I wanted was my tin of ravioli, thirty-seven pence. I even had the exact change ready. One twenty pence, one ten pence, one five pence and one two pence. Absolutely flawless transaction but I betted even this useless fucking snail of a till operator would find some way to stretch it out and fuck it up.

Finally, that's one customer done. Who even needs that many bags of lentils? A ridiculous amount. An unhealthy amount. Don't worry though, there were only four other customers with hefty loads to go. By this time, I felt I'd been here my whole life. I was hungry; this ravioli was all that I had. That thirty-seven pence was all I had. 'There should be a single till for people who only want one thing from the shop,' I kept going over this in my head. It made so much sense. I thought about a self-service checkout but I really hate the voice. You know, that condescending voice after everything you do. 'Place the item in the bagging area,' no, I'll place the item where I want. I felt people judging me about my purchase, especially the man behind me. Fuck do I care; anyone who is buying three tubs of Dairylea, but still feels the need to hide it under a 'That's OK' magazine couldn't possibly judge me, even in my fugue state. It's always funny watching people shit themselves in the bagging area – it's one where the cashiers don't help you put the items in the bag and the pressure's on when he starts lobbing things at you when there's no room left. Good times.

This man in question smelled like quiche. That's not good though, is it? I love a quiche but not when it's coming from old man pits. It's not his fault though, he was proper old, which to me is excusable. What's not excusable though is this absolute blue fart of a cashier was useless. It kept taking him a fucking age to scan anything – aye mate, keep turning it around slowly, that'll make a difference. Fuck sake.

What's that? 'Go easy on him?', 'He may have been really stressed as it was really busy?' No. I haven't finished ripping him apart yet. He needed to give someone change so he took out a bag of pennies from his till (who wants pennies anyways?) and his attempt to open it with his fingers didn't go to plan so he tried to gnaw it open. Nay luck. He looks around for an object to perhaps pry it open. Nay luck. He tries with his fingers again. Fucking hell man, we're stood watching this absolute clart desperately, fucking hysterically, trying to get this bag of pennies open. He turns to another member of staff sitting beside him on another aisle for assistance. 'Pass me a pen,' he says, clearly trying to keep his frustration from affecting the sound of his voice but didn't work; he ended up sounding like Gilbert Gottfried. He gets his pen and starts poking at it. Nay luck.

For goodness sake, does the customer really need her two pence that much? Now I'm angry at this woman who is stood watching him, no fucks given about the size of the queue; she was watching the world burn. Eventually she says 'forget it,' clearly to the man's glee, and we move to the next.

Finally, I'm next. I'm so close to ending this horrible shopping experience. I can taste my freedom... and my ravioli. Thirty-seven pence. I was next in the queue. I stepped up and handed him the ravioli; he didn't so much as flinch at the thought that I had been waiting so long for such a small product. He scans it and says 'thirty-seven pence please,' I couldn't move for the rage.

'Fuck sake, Connor, why has *that* annoyed you?'

It wasn't that it annoyed me, it was the fact that I had noticed something that I had never noticed before. The way he said it. He said it in like, a formal way, but totally forced it. It was as if a corporate of the supermarket was standing evaluating his performance and he forgot right up until serving me. 'thirty-seven pence place.' The inflexions on some of the words was the thing that got me. 'Thirty-*seven*,' then his tone goes higher for 'pence' then back down for 'please.' Am I the only person who picks up on shit like this? Aye probably.

Either that or he's just doing it to annoy me because he knows I've been watching him, swearing with anxiety. Because see when I said 'it's as if a corporate of the supermarket is next to him'? Yeah, he *wasn't*. So why is starting this bullshit now? Maybe he knows that I'm going to be home alone tonight, what with the ravioli; it doesn't exactly scream 'I'm having a massive blow-out with all of my mates tonight,' does it? Maybe he's giving me material for the book of short stories that I might end up writing.

But how does he know that? Is he some sort of stalker? Is he a clairvoyant? Who is this man who is pretending to be so bad at his job that it is completely noticeable? Well, if that'd that's the case, then why hasn't any of the other customers picked up on his ineptitude? His fuck ups are there for everyone to see, so why haven't they expressed any clear signs of exhaustion and frustration? Maybe they're a part of it; they're all a team to try and make my night better? Why would they do that? It's been about 45 seconds since he asked for my thirty-seven pence, I finally come back to earth when quiche man who is behind me, nudges me and says 'hurry up, lad.'

Performance Art Students

Stand the fuck up and stop blocking the corridors.

Stacey's Dream'

Stacey's obsession with Brief Encounter had always ran deep. You'd just need to quickly scan around her bedroom to know that. Not just her bedroom, you'd be able to see some kind of Brief Encounter memorabilia from anywhere in the house you stood. Posters, dolls, replicas, key rings and even paintings she'd attempted. She even had giant Brief Encounter spoke guards on her wheelchair, they were of the clock. And she loved that clock; she wanted nothing more than to visit the clock in Carnforth, Lancashire, before she died but at the age of 54 and riddled with diseases that don't allow her to walk or feel anything. If that wasn't enough, she lived in Brisbane, Australia, 10,238 miles away from Carnforth. It would never happen, it would stay a fantasy; something to dream about. What she'd give just to wheel up to that clock and look up at its magnificence and gaze into its history. No, she knew it was a pipe dream; it's her equivalent to winning the lottery or being in space. She had about seven of those clocks dangling around her house; the amount of ticking sounds around the house was incredible, it was the only notable sound around the place, other than Stacey's occasional humming of the Brief Encounter soundtrack.

It was tea time on a Friday afternoon in late November. Friday was a special day for Stacey, not only was it ravioli day, but that was the day where she would put the projector on for a cinematic viewing of Brief Encounter. Her ravioli was ready and the curtains were closed. It was 5.57pm, she could wait the three minutes until six on the dot – a nice round time to start, plus that way, with the film running for precisely ninety minutes, she'd know it'd be precisely half seven when it ends. With the projector being ready, she puts on the News to kill the time.

'It's been seventy years on the day since the most loved romantic film of all time come out,' says a reporter. Stacey nearly dropped her ravioli all over herself. Damien Quecks was the reporter, he and his shiny face was only in bloody Carnforth, next to the bloody clock. Magnifique. 'Because of the film's success, we're giving out free tickets for you to come to Carnforth and see the clock yourself, visit the museum and step foot into history.'

Holy smokes. Stacey couldn't believe it. By this time, she had wheeled herself towards the tele. December third as well, this was too much for her – she knew that December 3rd, 1972 was the first time she'd ever seen Brief Encounter because it was her mother's birthday. Quecks continues, 'all you have to do to win, is answer the question that follows and also write why you think it should be you. The question is: what is the name of the actor who plays Alec in the film?' Stacey manically grabs her laptop and starts typing. 'Send your answer and a little bit about yourself to QuecksComp@BrisbaneNews.aus and we'll be in touch. Good luck!'

Later that night, Stacey is tucked up in bed, smiling from ear to ear, teasing herself of the chances of winning the competition. 'Don't get ahead of yourself,' she thought, 'thousands of people would want a holiday to England.' She giggled. She didn't want to get to excited but she never had anything to look forward to. But actually, the film isn't that popular anymore. She wondered how many people would actually apply for it. She may get lucky; not only did she write the answer Trevor Howard, but included the second part of his surname, Smith, and his middle name Wallace... followed by 'I'm in a wheelchair.'

Stacey is now below the clock looking up at its magnificence and gazing into its history. She floats out of her wheelchair and floats towards it, the clock gets bigger as she shrinks into the three of the clock. She is now in the film, watching the final scene from above. She speaks the lines like her favourite song. She suddenly stops flying and falls into the ground then back out of the clock. She wakes with sweat gushing down her neck. What she'd give to receive a call from Damien Quecks.

A few days later, Stacey received a call from Damien Quecks. She squealed at his voice through the phone, not because she was a fan of Damien Quecks, quite the contrary, she found him repulsive and a condescending news anchor, she was squealing at the clock, for it was now all she could see. 'All your travel arrangements are paid for, you'll be starting with a bus into town this Friday, comfortable trains and planes AND on top of that, you'll get luxury accommodation.'

She begins packing. Throwing five different cameras into her case; she didn't need clothes. She threw in books and travel guides that she'd collected over the years of Carnforth; she knew the small town inside out, (Carnforth in Google Maps was bookmarked). Her case was packed, there was still lots of room but that was for souvenirs of course. She records her new answer phone message – 'I'm going to be away for a few days, it's finally happened. I'm going to see the clock.'

The last night before her big adventure, she couldn't sleep a wink, how could she? The time is 4.03am, she thinks about leaving extra early for her bus – four and a half hours early. The thought of missing that bus, oh no, she was going to see the clock and Stacey would never think about anything negative. She gets up, grabs her passport and wheels off.

At the bus stop, Stacey watches the sun rise behind her council estate. Her smile grows as the near-empty bus finally arrives. The doors throw themselves open revealing the stairway. Stacey wheels up to it, acknowledging the bus driver. The stocky man was gazing forward passed his steering wheel, he finally sees Stacey, who waves politely. He signs and winces, gets up, opens his bus driver door, bends down and opens up the ramp. What a chore! Stacey wheels herself up as best as she can but can't quite make it onto the bus. The driver, who was inches away from sitting back down throws a silent tantrum. He returns to the front of the bus and forcefully shoves Stacey on the bus. 'Where you goin'?' he grunts. Stacey wheels up to the driver and puts her pass on the scanner. 'What a horrible man,' Stacey thought. What a damp start to the day and what a bad mood he put Stacey in. No, she was going to see the clock and Stacey wouldn't let herself think about anything negative.

The bus was an extremely bumpy one, Stacey had to have a tight hold of the complementary bars or she'd be rocking all over the place like the dodgems! The bus was approaching a roundabout, just outside the airport. The airport, Stacey watched a plane rising from the back of the building, just in a few hours she'd be- CRACK. That's a bump on the head for Stacey. What's your bet the bus driver did that on purpose?

Finally, Stacey is off the bus from hell, she didn't say thank you when exiting at first but she wanted to keep a positive attitude so she did. She turns after exiting the bus only to see the bus doors closing in her face. Goodness me, why did this bus driver hate Stacey? Never mind. She wheels up to the airport, checks in and, you're joking... her flight is delayed. Only by an hour, Stacey could wait, she'd just watch Brief Encounter in her head. She got up to the final scene; 'if you die, you'd forget me. I want to be remembered,' she mouths along to the final words of Alec, with tears rolling down her face. The soundtrack aloud in her head ends abruptly as a voice from the tannoy sounds: 'calling flight 261 to Manchester, England,' – this was hers, Stacey lit up. 'We're sorry to announce that flight 261 to Manchester, England has been cancelled in result of bad weather conditions, we have rescheduled a duel-flight to Chicago that will call at Manchester. The flight will be at 17.04 at terminal 6C.' Good heavens, that's only another six hours to wait, or four showings of Brief Encounter. Fiddlesticks.

Hours (and showings) had passed. Stacey had fallen asleep. The tannoy smugly announces the last call for flight 261. Stacey stays asleep, muttering Brief Encounter related words; even the name Damien Quecks came up. Everyone had left the terminal, Stacey hadn't. Some of the flight attendants and staff became aware of her. 'Should we go and see where she's going?' one of them asked. They approach Stacey who is still muttering. 'Damien... Quecks... Damien... Damien...' The flight attendants attempt to wake her up but to no avail. 'She's not waking up,

Priscilla, is she dead?' one of them asks with trepidation. 'Damien…Damien,' 'Oh thank god, what's she saying? Is it Yemen?' 'Yeah, it sounds like Yemen. Maybes that's where she's going.'

More hours pass. Stacey wakes up on the plane; it's crammed. Specks of light burst in through the window followed by a roar of thunder. Stacey had never flown before so she didn't know what was going on. 'Is this what it's like all of the time!?' she wondered. The plane shakes, thrusting her to one side on her neighbour. 'Sorry,' she cries, the woman next to her apologies in a foreign language; Stacey didn't know which. She hears worried muttering around her, again in a different language. The captain starts making an announcement, again in a different language, then the same announcement in ANOTHER language. A stewardess rushes by, Stacey tries to grab her attention – 'excuse me, I think I'm on the wrong flight,' the stewardess carries on down the aisle and plonks down on her seat, throwing the seat belt on her. She looks at Stacey and shakes her head; eyes open the whole time. The captain continues, he finally gets to English: 'Preparing to emergency landings with this weather danger.' Stacey squeals. The plane descends to the ocean. Crash.

Months had passed this time. Stacey had begun a new life in the heart of Socotra Island; an island that festered with wildlife and tribes. Luckily for Stacey, the tribes had taken to her. Well, more than that, they thought she was something of a goddess; it was the way she crawled about the place. They gave her food and gifts which mainly consisted of necklaces made from a gathering of Mishhahir flowers. This was a lifestyle she got used to very quickly; her Carnforth replica watch stopped long ago.

Stacey quickly became aware of the politics of her tribe, named 'The Guabalajees', and how there was an imminent war with their rival tribe, named 'The Imps'. Stacey and her army were ready; the spears were sharpened and the pebbles were ready to throw, first call was sunrise. Stacey treated them to a special meal before bedtime: crab ravioli, which she called Crabioli. All the ingredients were easy enough to get, apart from the crab which she had to persuade the fisherman to acquire. Everyone seemed to love it; it was a fine cuisine compared to their usual rice and Feki fruit salad. They dined and went to sleep, Stacey is the last to go to bed; she sits and looks into the fire, dreading the dawn. Her eyes close.

A loud horn sounds. Stacey jumps up not next to a fire but a dog tied to a chair on a ship deck. It barks, seemingly offended at Stacey, who crawls away from it and towards the end of the vessel. She peers over and looks beyond the miles and miles of dark blue water. 'Are you alright?' asks a man approaching her with a tray of food consisting of a glass of water, slices of pineapple and a bowl of Shredded Wheat. He places it down next to her, 'we picked you up on that island because you were twitching.' Stacey picks up the water and necks it. 'What about my tribe? What about the war? I don't like pineapple,' she exclaims as she gasps for air. 'The tribes were dead, they fought overnight, although most of them died due to food poisoning.' Stacey wondered how one can tell if someone dies from food poisoning. 'You're on a Voyager cruise ship now, we'll take you straight to a hospital as soon as we get back to London.' 'That's in England! Is it near Carnforth?' Stacey demanded. The man shrugged. 'We'll go wherever you want to go as soon as you're all clear.' A grin became etched on her face. 'Get some rest,' the man said politely. Stacey's eyes closed.

There was a loud explosion nearby. Stacey jumped up. 'PIRATES!!!' bellowed a member of the crew. Gangs of Somalian pirates had raided the ship, equipped with guns. They gathered the people aboard the ship to the main cabin and explained they were taking the ship to 'get money.' Stacey couldn't imagine how they'd get money after taking so many hostages. She cleared her throat and asked the pirates. 'Excuse me, Mr Pirate?' – it was sensible to be as polite as possible. 'No talk! Stand with the others!' Pirate number one said. 'Oh, I can't. I don't have any legs.' He doesn't understand. He looks down at Stacey, his jaw drops. He scurries to his pirate colleague and whispers in Somalian. There is a silence then an agreement. He comes back to Stacey. 'You lucky. Blackfoot where we go for you.' Stacey couldn't imagine who or what Blackfoot was. To her, it sounded like a big, bad pirate lord, even worse than pirate number one, who was devilishly tall.

Stacey was treat very well compared to the other hostages who weren't fed at all. She was given very good meals and got to know the pirates. Pirate number one's name was actually Steve. He told the pirates about her journey and about Brief Encounter. She had assigned them parts to play in their own rendition of the film that they performed to keep the hostages happy – Brief Encounter Somalia was its name.

Months had passed and Stacey wanted to go home. She had been away for the best part of a year. Her hair was much longer now and forgot what the land looked like. Every day that passed was another day closer to seeing Blackfoot. As close as she became to the pirates, they wouldn't tell her who or what it was. But today was special. Steve approached her and said 'Blackfoot today,' the ship stopped suddenly, he continues 'Blackfoot now.' Shortly after, Stacey is carried out by Steve, she looks up the pier and up at a tower. 'This isn't Blackfoot, this is Blackpool!' Steve then drugs Stacey and takes her to a secret location.

Stacey wakes up in a hospital bed. There is a doctor standing over her smiling. He is not very pirate-looking. 'You will be worth a fortune now,' He says quickly. Stacey looks down. Robot legs. *Robot* legs. She stands up, wobbling everywhere. 'You're not selling me, old man,' She spits. She kicks him to the ground and begins running away...backwards. 'You fool. Did you honestly think I would programme you to be able to walk in the conventional way?' That's alright, she could walk backwards. She wasn't used to walking forwards any more than walking backwards so there was no problem.

She could run so fast. Albeit backwards but she was using a mirror that she found in the doctor's surgery as a reference for direction. It was only so many miles to Carnforth from Blackpool. She'd be there in no time. She hadn't stopped thinking about the clock; it was the only thing keeping her going; the belief that she'd one day lay her eyes upon it. Stacey finally saw a sign for Carnforth – 15 miles! She just wanted to get there, no more pirates, no more tribes, no more islands, just the clock; 4 miles away now! She could smell the mechanics from the clock, or maybe it was her legs giving way; she was gradually getting slower and slower. Finally, she stood still, then collapsed. She looks up at a sign: 'Carnforth – one mile.' She was so close; she grabs a rock from next to her and bashes the legs off. 'If I have to crawl, I'll crawl.' And she did.

Hours later, Stacey found herself in an abandoned train yard. Was this the right place? She crawled like a frigid mouse, running to its warm abode. The rain crashes down so she takes shelter in the back of one of the trains. 'This doesn't look like anything in the film, oh God, I've come all this way for nothing.' At least Stacey had learnt a valuable lesson on her trip: don't rely on public transport. She sniggered then, a bolting loud whistle echoed around the train yard. She leaps out and follows the sound. The whistle gradually gets louder as she gets closer. 'Oh my goodness', there it was. A very small station and...the clock. It's beautiful. Stacey can't take her eyes off it. She crawled up to the clock, looked up at its magnificence and gazed into its history.

She must have been looking at it for a good hour; reviewing her journey and wondering if it was worth it. 'Just look at it, of course it is.' 'Excuse me, are you all right?' asks a man in chef whites. Stacey explains her wild endeavours to her new friend. 'Christ Almighty, that's amazing. Would you like to see the Brief Encounter museum?' Stacey held out her arm and the man pulled her up.

Stacey was sat on a brand new wheelchair observing anything and everything in the small museum. Film canisters, pictures of the cast and crew and real life props from the film. She was in heaven. A door opens in the corner of the room and a man walks out followed by a small crowd of people. 'The next screening is now.' Stacey wheeled herself along to the room, which turns out to be a mini theatre; it looked very posh, mind. The film began with a montage of the best parts of the film and different 'making-of' shorts. Euphoria. Then the clock was spoken about in enormous detail. Oh, the clock. What didn't Stacey know about the clock? She thought she knew everything. A man came on the screen and gave a few interesting facts about it.

'In actual fact, the clock has deteriorated over time and has been changed with different parts and faces so many times, that it isn't actually the real clock anymore. The real clock parts have either been sold or discarded.' Stacey's smile faded into disbelief. Her excitement turned into anger. Into rage. She furiously wheeled along to the organiser of the film and asked: 'Excuse me, that part about the clock...is it true?' He nodded. Stacey slumps into melancholy. 'So, I came all this way... for nothing?'

She wheels out in a sombre state. All this way for a plastic mockery. What else could she do with her life now? She couldn't get back to Brisbane; she'd no money! Stacey knew that, although with a disappointing climax, her adventure was fun but it had to end here. She rolled up to a train platform, observed the sign 'Lancaster – 10.47'. The time was 10.46. She kissed her Brief Encounter watch and threw herself onto the train tracks.

Minutes pass, Stacey sighs and looks up to the digital clock; the time was now 10.51. A voice echoes from a nearby speaker, 'Calling passengers for the 10.47 train to Lancaster on platform 3, we regret to say that this train has been cancelled for a malfunction on the tracks.'

Mid-Twenties Syndrome

There's a part of me that can only be accessed by inducing a specific amount of alcohol, being in a particular place and having day with a decency rating of less than 35%. I'm of course talking about being pissed in a club and analytically dissecting everyone and everything. I swear to fuck; I think I'm Sherlock Holmes in this scenario. Proper on the ball. What I tend to do though, is log these thoughts in a sort of digital, drunken slur on my phone. Going through these the morning after is both confusing and hilarious. I just want to document them here and try and summarise what I was talking about when I'm trying to be fucking Ghandi.

Sitting with your mate. A phone vibrates, you check your phone and it's not yours, it's your mate's. (08/01/2015 22:14)

Errmm, aye....and? Do you want to finish that fucking statement, Con? I was probably annoyed at how unpopular I am. Or maybe, this was a result to suppress embarrassment that the text wasn't for me and this is a pretend text to some cunt? Spot on.

Fog machines GAN off unwarranted. (16/01/2015 22:45)

This was at a friend's gig. I think I was stoned when writing this actually because I remember laughing at the price of onion rings earlier that night. There was an acoustic act before the band and the guy playing was singing fucking The Smiths or some depressing shite. It was a melancholic song to say the least and in the midst of it, a fog machine went off, supposedly for effect. I suppose I thought it was funny. Also snuck in a tin of Mulligatawny soup to that club. Banter.

Girls and jackets. (15/02/2015 02:01)

I'm not 100% but I think I was referring to the act of giving a lassy a jacket, lest her be cold, and then for her to give it you back to get another jacket from the lad she likes. Just passed two as well, brutal time.

Shitting a house out. (16/03/2015 05:56)

Bloody six in the morning. Christ, I'm some kind of mental boy. I can never remember really ever needing a shit in a club during a night out. Aye it happens but we're always really prepared for our pish-ups (piss-ups). However, when you're a crazy cat like me and go out all-night long, you definitely brew up some sizes of litter, in this case the size of a house, that will have to wait for its time to christen the pan.

The hole in a shirt that you put your arm in is called an 'arms aye'. (25/06/2015 18:44)

I cannot remember writing this one but I hope it's true. If not, I will refer to the holes in shirts that you put your arms in as 'arms aye's from this moment on wards. And you should too.

The bouncer told u to put ur shoe on. (12/08/2015 00:01)

I actually lost my phone this night. I was talking to a lass in very loud club via the notes on my phone and this is the only one that was left. I let her hold my phone while I went for a piss. Why? Fuck knows. Nothing happened though, she left and handed it in behind the bar. Why did I take my shoes off? Maybes I was looking for my phone.

I'm not drunk enough for this. (02/09/2015 01:28)

I don't get this one. I just don't. What wasn't I drunk enough for? Dancing? Talking? If so, why did I write it? I must've been somewhat tipsy to write something, but what is the purpose? It doesn't mean anything! Fuck sake, Connor, IT DOESN'T MEAN ANYTHING.

Right, some absolute cunt with the bare minimum of effort for a Halloween custume came as a cat. First of all, why is he a cat and second, why is he having a go at my costume. Wearing trackie bottoms with two stripes as well the fuckin smurf (31/10/2015 00:29)

Yeah, he was a pure gimp. Drew whiskers on himself the absolute fucking sponge cake. It was quite strange actually, this was at a house party and nobody knew who he was and why he was there. His soul purpose was to gate crash and insult me. I remember him walking in the room and asking why I was dressed as an elf. I said "because it's Halloween, why are you dressed like a cunt?" I think I had a decent point to be fair.

That photo. An experiment. A drink on the edge like you. (31/10/2015 02:11)

I have a photograph on my phone of a double vodka & coke on the edge of a bench surrounded by straws and other spillages. I can only assume that these two come hand in hand. Cryptic as ever. 'A drink on the edge like you'. Like who? I don't know anyone who resembles a drink.

You're gona feel like a cunt when you are sober but finding a lost coin in a fiver just shows. (11/11/2015 03:16)

I was right about one thing.

One of them cunts who are aThen (14/11/2015 22:43)

I know exactly what I meant here and didn't correct the mistake so I would remember staring at the person in question when writing. He always tried to one-up me. "Oh, I've has a PS4 for ages" or "Oh, my dad's really tall". Haven't seen him since.

Girls and Boys by goodCharlotte (21/11/2015 00:54)

Speaks for itself. On the heavy metal floor of a club, I wanted to see if the DJ would put that on. He didn't.

And that's all I have in my phone. I will no doubt continue this trend where I think I'm being profound but I'm in fact being a knob. I wrote them out exactly how they appear on my phone which is why the grammar is shite. Might start writing equations when I'm steaming, one of them could be the meaning of life. Deep, that.

The Joke

The joke came to me in my sleep on a Winter's evening in 2014. I wasn't sleeping very well at that moment because 2014 wasn't a very kind year to me for a few reasons. This joke probably saved my life. It gave me, not only luxurious sleep for a long while after that, but a great laugh that I tried to share with my friends. It fills me with joy and even more so when I share it with strangers on the street. The reaction to the joke has been phenomenal.

I love comedy and I love bringing joy to people so whenever I can extract bad moods from people and replace it with happy, kind times, it's amazing. I like to try and adapt to people's humour depending on who I'm with and I like to think I do that successfully unless I'm just not as funny as them; in this case I just try and learn to be a funnier and ultimately a better person.

The joke resembles a friendly cat, but he doesn't have an owner; one of those cats who surreptitiously lurks around the estate, hiding under cars. Nervous, but not afraid of interaction. The cat is a free spirit, just like the joke. But, actually, not many people like those cats. My dad always shouts at next door's cat when it's in the garden...

Here's the thing, I wasn't entirely honest about the reception of that joke. When I said that got a phenomenal reaction, it didn't. I'd say that it got mixed reviews – like if my joke was on a review website, it would get around 46% and that's being generous because they were mainly pity laughs from my family. People actually said I was a cunt for telling them the joke. They'd be like 'Connor, I don't need any more reasons to dislike you and you're coming out with shite like that. Now get out of my garden.'

I bet you're dying to hear (read) the joke so I'm going to put it down below. Consider this publication a courier for its suicide. This joke will never be uttered by anyone again because it's *that* average. Upon reading this joke, you will think nothing of it and will probably regret reading it – that's why I have decided to offer an explanation for it. Goodbye joke, you were a very special thing in my life but now, it is time for your demise. The joke is as follows.

What does the England football team get if they work four days a week?

Three lie ins.

Russell's Ices

Everyone loved Russell because of his trademark thumbs up to everyone he passes in his big, blue ice cream van. He was so friendly, basically on a first-name basis with all the kids and their parents. He was one of those people who was consistently happy; he always brightened up your day, even if it was shit. God forbid anyone seeing Russell in a stinky mood, nobody would know what it would look like.

Russell was great at hiding his true problems; he was in massive debt and his job as a job as an ice cream man would never be able to cover it. He didn't care, he loved his job too much – he moved into a cheap, shit hole of a flat. It's not like he had a family to support, or that much of a social life but he still needed to find a way to get out of his financial shit-bastard.

His only choice would be to use his van as a courier for drugs, why get another job when he can do two at once? He would pick up a brand new ice lolly called Mr Bubble, which was a blueberry lolly with a very powerful drug in it – it was all the rage, then he'd have to drive it to a location and exchange the product for cash. Nobody would suspect him because of his status among the locals. It had been a long time coming, he was hassled by drug lords many times in the past to try and acquire his services but he would turn them away. His hands were tied though, how else could he pay his debt? He was about to be evicted from his shit hole of a flat, that would be the lowest of the low!

Russell didn't specifically know what drug it was, he didn't want any knowledge of it other than where to take it and how much he was getting. People were beginning to identify that something wasn't right with Russell, his thumbs ups weren't as frequent and he didn't seem as chipper as usual; always checking his phone when children would try to talk to him. It was his first day as a criminal so he was constantly on edge. He does his usual round a couple of hours after school. One of his most successful spots was in the estate, next to the park; kids would pile up against the van once they hear his famous ice cream van jingle. One child in particular, named Tommy, peers over the hatch when he gets to the front, 'What's that?' he asks, pointing at a large stack of boxes labelled Mr. Bubble. 'Oh, nothing, son,' he dismisses but Tommy is keen to know. Russell had known Tommy and his family for quite some time; he was good friends with Tommy's grandad. 'Is it a new lolly? Can I please try it?' he politely requests. 'Sorry lad, it's a special delivery and the man would be quite upset if one was missing,' Russell softballs. 'Oh kaayyyy,' Tommy continues, 'can I just have a 99 with monkey's blood please,' 'course you can.' Thank god that's over. After Tommy traipses away, Russell goes to the stack of boxes and moves them out of sight.

After serving the last child, Russell's shift was over – it was now time to wait for the big exchange. He was terrified; he hadn't ever met these wrong-doers before, only spoke to one of them on the phone. He was in no position to call anybody a wrong-doer though, especially after this. Was he doing the right thing? Probably not but everyone has their dark moments. He checks his phone once more - one new message.

'Ten minutes,' it read. He drives to an abandoned car repair garage. He parks and waits for someone and they took their time; a man finally taps on his window. He presses a button on his dashboard to make the window go down but then the ice cream van jingle comes on. 'Do you fucking mind? We're trying to be a bit low-key here, turn it off,' the man says abruptly. 'Buggeration, sorry,' he slams the buttons on the dashboard, it finally stops. He looks out his rear view mirror, expecting his view to be blocked by the boxes he moved but it isn't, the boxes had been moved slightly. 'Your back door is locked; would you mind?' the man asks. Russell twists his face, 'it shouldn't be locked,' he turns and jumps in the back of the van – Mr. Bubble wrappers everywhere, empty. Blue residue slopped across his van, some half-eaten lollies remained; there was a trail of litter leading up to an incapacitated child – *it was Tommy*.

He takes about forty seconds to process what he is looking at. 'Anytime you like, pal,' he can hear. Russell returns to the front and looks around in a haze. The man nods at another man stood at the other side of the van, the door is still locked. He sighs, 'look, I know you're nervous but the sooner we get this done, the better,' he whispers.

So many things were going through Russell's mind – he couldn't give the drugs to the drug men because most of the drugs were gone, he couldn't take the child back home because the child was extremely drugged up and he couldn't take the child to the police because, well, the child was extremely drugged up. The best thing to do? Russell slams the keys in the ignition and speeds off, the men scream after him and revert to their vehicles to begin the chase the ice cream van, which blares out the jingle once more.

Tommy sprouts up, he walks to the front of the moving van. 'Russell, *that...*' – '*Tommy!* I'm so sorry lad, are you alright? Sit down, put a seatbelt or something,' Russell is overwhelmed with things to say. '...*that* was the best lolly I've ever had,' Tommy says laconically. Russell radically turns around tight corners as a couple of Fiat Puntos are close on his tail. 'I'll get you home, don't worry, you'll be alright,' Russell says desperately. 'I don't want to go home yet, Russell, everything's bubbly,' says Tommy waving his hand in front of his face. 'Oh Christ, Tommy, how many did you have, son?' asks Russell – '*loads,*' he answers, 'they taste really nice but they make me feel reaaaally funny,' he starts giggling. 'That's because they're really old and not meant to be eaten. They're very bad for you,' says Russell, frequently looking around. The evil Fiat Puntos corner the van off, forcing him to take a turn into an estate. 'There's my house!' shouts Tommy, Russell looks over and sees a house surrounded in police cars. 'Oh buggar,' he chokes. The police cars light up red and blue and suddenly chase after him with the words 'pull over,' echoing from a megaphone. Russell has to break through garden fences to escape both contrarieties.

So there's a drugged up bairn in the back, Russell is wanted for property damages and kidnapping and to top it off, an entire drug mafia are after him for stealing expensive goods. Wey that's less than fucking stellar.

Connor's Recipe

This is how I make my signature dish. I call it 'Slow-Cooked Spiffing Mutton.' It is very much inspired by the Tongonese way of cooking. Pay close attention and follow these steps carefully because you could end up with a fine mess should you miss out key details. It is very much an old, family recipe; I remember Mam and Dad arguing about how much lentils you need for the perfect mutton. My Dad always uses 6 bags but Mam, the silly witch, uses 5. Laughable.

Ingredients
1 X Sheep Mutton
3 X Onions
2 X Bottles of Corona
1 X Jar of Pickle Brine
6 X Eggs
1 X Banana
1 X Lettuce
1 X Basil (for garnish)
1 X Tube of Primula Cheese & Chive
1 X Pack of Doritos Roulette
Loads and loads of Lentils (5 bags)

Step one:

Open the Doritos and scran them as you cook. Warm up the belly. Put them in a bowl if you like but I just eat them from the packet. Or you could just save them for pudding. It's up to you, do what you want – *you're an adult.* Don't try and be clever and add a few crisps in the pot with the other stuff. It-will-ruin-it.

Step two:

Shave the onion of its dry exterior and cut holes in the middle of the onion so it looks like a little peep-hole. You don't need to use a knife for the hole, just give it a little pokey pokey and the bottom should just pop out, like a dad dropping his children off for school. Cut the banana into thirds and stuff the banana into the onion. Get it right in there and shave off the ends so it is fully stuffed. Turn the slow cooker on to the 'low' setting and place your banonions into the pot. Pour a bottle of Corona into the slow cooker, followed by loads of lentils and the Primula cheese.

Step three:

Dice your lettuce into tiny bits, put in another pot with the other Corona and boil it. Boil it so hard. Add an egg. Add another egg. Add three more eggs and then add the pickle brine. Don't throw away the egg-shells, either. The chickens went through hell for those eggs and you're just gonna bin them? Get something and bash them into smithereens and add it to the mix. This is going to stink but if you want to take the train, you've got to buy the ticket.

Step four:

Oh I forgot to tell you to add the Sheep mutton to the onions and bananas. Leave it for eight hours. Keep boiling the lettuce and eggs for eight hours on a low heat. Let it simmer by putting a lid on it or the chopping board that you used or another pan or anything. Make sure you wash up after yourself; unsanitary sheep mutton – this is not.

Step five:

After eight hours, return to your collection of bullshit. Get a plate out, drain the onions and mutton using a cauldron, drain the lettuce and eggs using a cauldron and place them on to the plate. Garnish with one egg (raw) and the rest of lentils. It usually serves up to four people but if you're hungry, you could eat what you can, tub it up and have it for a packed lunch the day after! Enjoy!

The Mayans are Coming

Shaun's nightshift had just begun. He strolled into the garden centre, rolling his eyes at the amount of unorganized boxes of shit he would have to go through. He sulks, booting several of the empties across the room. He wanders in to the staff room where Rob is sat reading a newspaper. 'Oh my god, have you seen this? Someone has actually grown their leg back,' he says in awe. Shaun groans; it's too early for this. 'Aye, right,' he mumbles as he makes a cuppa. 'Honestly, they're doing tests because they think he might be part-lizard,' Shaun peaks at the front page. 'I wouldn't take much notice of what The Sun are printing to be honest,' Rob's amazement is unscathed.

In the stock room, Shaun grabs a large box of batteries but Rob stops him. 'We need to *count* all this,' Shaun sighs 'Why? Can we not just guess it?' 'No, you say that every week. It needs to be done properly. Get a pen and paper and start with the fish,' demands Rob. 'Oh so *I'm* doing them this week?' teases Shaun. Last week Rob tried to put too many fish in to one bag, it burst and flooded the stock room. He remembers the sight of 50 rainbow fish surfing under the door into the customer section and hearing the screams of children.

Shaun mutters numbers at complete random as he ticks off things on his clipboard. Rob is fiddling with the radio, trying to get a clear signal. 'This happens every week, I can never get it to work,' Shaun puts down his clipboard, walks up to the radio and puts the antenna up, 'Yeah, it does happen every week cause you're a fucking idiot,' Shaun sighs. Rob snaps 'don't talk to your boss like that,' Shaun scoffs. The radio is now working; an announcer gives an announcement, slowly and concise.

'We're under attack. The Mayans. The Mayans are coming. After another failed prediction for the end of the world, they've decided to end it themselves so that one of their prophecies will finally come true. They are here, in Great Britain. They've killed hundreds with their spears. They are showing no mercy. They've taken down Big Ben and moved up north as far as Yorkshire. They are erasing us one by one.'

'Oh my God!' squeals Rob. He squeezes the drill that he's holding against his chest. 'If anyone is still out there,' the announcer continues 'please be aware that the enemy are mainly equipped with large spears and poisonous blow darts.' 'What about the army!? Why haven't they been called!? Shouldn't the army have done something!?' Rob continues to hysterically shriek. 'Be quiet, I'm trying to listen.' Shaun giggles, clearly entertained at Rob's whiney voice. The announcer continues.

'We're expecting towns to be evacuated in the coming minutes, starting with large towns in the North East of England.' He pauses, 'Er, I'm just being told that we'll be starting *up* and then working *down* the country. We'll be escorting people to safety in Luxembourg where fortifications have been prepared. In order to evacuate citizens accordingly, we will mark your door with either a red cross or a green cross. The red crosses will be evacuated in the AM and the green crosses the PM. County Durham will-'

Shaun laughs 'Howay man, that's a fucking *shite* idea.' Rob frantically begins to ask questions – 'What if I have a red door and they mark it red? *How will I know!?*' being some of them. 'Then you'll get left behind,' 'But Shaun, how will they know? You're not taking this seriously, *be more scared!*' 'Ah come on, it's bollocks. You've probably found some random-arse station where some lonely old man is broadcasting from his shed.' Rob takes a minute to think. 'Then why have they got the Red Cross involved then?' Shaun laughs some more 'I don't think that fighting Mayans is on the Red Cross' mission statement, mate.' 'Well what about us? How will they know we're here, we've only got shutters! Tell us!' He furiously shakes the radio for more information. Shaun attempts to restrain him. The radio flies across the room from their scrap and breaks into pieces. The radio utters its last words – 'County Durha-'

'Oh my god, what about Durham? *What about Durham!?*' screams Rob. He pathetically tries to piece together the clearly destroyed radio. He pats his pocket then looks at Shaun, who watches him in astonishment. 'I've not got my phone, you got yours? Get on the news or something and find out what's going on,' 'Oh come on. You actually think it's fucking real?' Rob stood abashed. Shaun shakes his head – 'We can't use our phones because of the blocker.' The blocker was a device that Boss Daniels installed in his office so that employees were not to be, in his words, 'distracted by the bigger picture.' 'We need to go and turn it off then. Daniels will understand, it's about safety!' Rob pleads. 'Do you honestly believe that?' scoffs Shaun, Rob nods. 'So, since you're my 'superior', you're saying it's OK to break into Boss-man's office?' Rob nods – 'come with me, I'm scared.'

Shaun is stood outside an office. The door, which reads 'Mr. Michaels', is closed with a pass code required to open. Rob peaks his head around the corner. Shaun tries combination after combination. 'Come on, think. Has he got a pet or something?' he asks. Rob stutters. 'You're the one who wanted to get in here. Get it together. You have a go, I'm out of ideas.' Shaun moves aside for Rob, who slowly approaches the door. 'Oh, just get on it for fuck sake.' Shaun pushes Rob towards the door and then leaves. 'I'll be right back,' he shouts. Rob sits down next to the door; he knows *everything* about Boss Michaels - from all of his pet's names to his favourite Rolling Stones song. 'It's not Sympathy for the Devil,' he mutters. He had tried all sorts. The date his dog was born, nope. The date his son lost his first tooth, not that. It wasn't his favourite brand of deodorant – Lynx Apollo it was not! It wasn't even 18:44 23052013 which was the time and date Boss Michael's first son was conceived. He was out of ideas. But suddenly, a brain wave hits him. 'I know it!' – 'Watch it,' shouts Shaun. Rob turns to see Shaun sprinting towards the door with a massive set of wireless garden strimmers. Rob dives out of the way, the door is destroyed. 'We're in.'

'Are you stupid!? Do you know how much that'll cost!? I'll have to put a call out now,' Rob stresses. 'Yeah out a call out, I'm sure *that'll* be their priority. It's an emergency anyways,' Shaun says derisively, he throws the stimmers down and takes out a sledge hammer which he has equipped on his back. 'Where's this jammer? There it is!' He charges towards the corner and starts smashing objects on the desk. 'Shaun, no! That's a picture of his family,' Shaun stops – 'Might've be hidden.' – 'No, it's like a box. Where could it be?' asks Rob as he looks in the cupboard containing various uniforms. 'Here it is,' whispers Shaun. He's standing next to his desk and kicks underneath it – out flies a mini satellite. They look upon its sacred commodity.

Shaun begins smashing the absolute fuck out of it. Rob hesitates – 'But, what if they can find us?' Shaun stops and considers, 'Yeah but, surely if there's a *signal*, they'd be able to triangulate the position right now. So, I'm actually...destroying the signal?' There is a long silence. 'I'm not sure how it works actually, fuck it,' Rob admits. Shaun continues to smash.

*

Across the road is a John Lewis which is closed. Police had lately been booking out the stock room for hostage negotiation training because 'there's nowhere else,' the sergeant would sternly explain. About twenty police officers jog around to warm up, ten are dressed in civilian clothes and the other ten are in police uniform. 'GATHER UP!' bellows the sergeant. The troops form an orderly line. They're beginning to go through the correct protocols in a hostage situation. The ten dressed in civilian clothes stay put while the others line up at the other side of the room, one of the 'civilians' hides behind some plasma TV's – 'No no, go somewhere else, we don't want to add to the budget.' He obeys and creeps behind somewhere else instead. The policemen get into position and the room is silent. 'I'LL BLOW HIS FUCKING HEAD OFF!' screams the fake hostage-taker behind the microwaves. One policeman, Jason, steps up. 'Just, uh, please don't,' his voice filled with dismay, the kind of dismay where he'd clearly been up all night worrying about this training. 'Okay, enough,' demands the sergeant. Jason halts – 'w-what was wrong this time?' he whimpers. ''Please don't', *Please don't*'? This guy has just said he's going to blow his *ahem* *fucking head* off, well said by the way,' he acknowledges the fake hostage taker, 'and *you* say 'please don't?' You need to get into their head, understand *why*. If you say 'please don't' like that, he'll know he's in control.' Straight after the sergeant finishes, sirens blare from outside. The police officers react and run out.

The horn is being blasted and the lights are flashing blue and red. The police come pouring out of John Lewis and approach the hijacked police car. It's kids. Just kids. The police crowd around it, but the kids escape, laughing about their vigilant reckoning. The sergeant watches from the door and walks towards them slowly 'whose car is that?' The squad fall silent. 'It's car number 23, *whose-is-car-23*?' Jason hides behind his colleagues.

'You left your car unlocked?' the sergeant has Jason pinned down, *mentally*. 'I'm sorry!' Jason bursts out. 'To be honest, I think I'm more disappointed at how you handled the situation. There was a potential commandeering of your government-licensed vehicle and you just let them run away,' the sergeant continues. 'Y-yeah, but they were just kids.' – '*They could've been dwarves,*' He hisses back. The other officers fight back laughter. 'Since this man is having a bit of a rough morning, I think we should go easy on him.' Jason takes a sigh of relief. '...after he runs a raid,' The officers gasp, Jason pleads. 'Please no, I've hardly done any raids,' 'Well, it's time you got started.'

'Shaun, stop!' Shaun stops. 'Do you hear that?' Shaun hears that. 'Oh my god, the police are here to save us,' the siren dies down, Shaun and Rob dash towards the office window. They see a group of people pointing their guns at police officers. They see the sergeant shouting something inaudible and they go inside John Lewis. 'Oh no! The Mayans have got them,' Shaun's smile fades. 'Holy shit, it's real,' he mutters. He bolts out of the room and into the main garden centre. He grabs a trolley and throws in strips of wood flooring, drills, nails and ladders. He starts fortifying the main doors, Rob tries to lend a hand but Shaun keeps waving him away. 'If you want to help, make yourself useful and start boarding up the windows and doors. I'm going to start making weapons.' – 'With what?' – 'Look around.'

Shaun races through the aisles, using his trolley as a scooter at times. He loads it with everything: ladders, wood, drills, shears and even some garden gnomes. He wheels passed one of those commercial things where they are mega-excited about the shittest things. 'Try this brand new 'Kill 'em Dead' fertilizer. All new from 'Kill 'em Dead'. Spray your sorry weeds with this extremely flammable pesticide and live your life in piece,' says a well-groomed man putting on a shite American accent for some reason. Shaun loads his trolley with it.

Back at the staff room, Rob is trying to get a signal on his phone. Shaun enters 'That was the worst craftsmen ship ever, have you never barricaded yourself into a garden centre before?' Rob stands his phone up on a desk. 'Please send help to Daniel's Home Store. We're under attack by the Mayans,' Rob pleads. 'Look, Rob!' Shaun shows off a rake with chisel tied on the end. – 'We've tried to fortify the perimeter and salvaged weapons with what we have. Please help.' Rob takes the phone off the table and fiddles with it for a bit and then... 'Oh no, upload failed,' Shaun realises what he's doing. 'No no, if we're making a distress video thing, it needs to be better than that!'

Shaun stands revving a chainsaw with a gas mask on. 'HOWAY THEN, MAYANS!' he shouts righteously. Rob stands timidly behind him squeaking 'Help. Please help.' Shaun continues screaming, he takes out a hose and squirts fertilizer towards the window 'BRING IS THE LIGHTER, ROB! BRING IS THE LIGHTER!' Rob obeys and lights a spark, the liquid erupts, smashing through the window. 'SHIT! TURN IT OFF, TURN IT OFF!!!' The video ends, Rob immediately tries to board up the window. 'Wait actually, hold your phone out the window and try uploading that.'

*

Jason wipes the sweat of his face as he walks out of John Lewis, he is followed closely by the Sergeant. 'Good job son, you've redeemed yourself. I should think can run operations now,' Jason blushes 'Oh, I'm not sure about that, sir.' – 'No, come on. The next situation is all yours.' The sergeant pats Jason on the back. Flames burst out of the building opposite, followed by screaming. The police take cover behind their vehicles. 'WHAT THE FUCK IS THAT!?' bellows the fake-hostage taker. They watch the window, shortly after, a small hand peaks out holding a phone and after a few seconds, the hand accidentally drops the phone. 'Jason, you can run this operation. I need to get intel.' The sergeant says, he goes to his car and speaks into the radio. 'WHAT DO WE DO, JASON!?' demands the fake-hostage taker. Jason points to the building 'Let's, er, let's go and check it out.' Many of the officer's murmur, 'Jason, we can't just go and see because we don't know the extent of the threat,' the sergeant returns 'We have a hostage situation, line up accordingly. The only intel I have is a YouTube link. Gather round.' They watch the video.

They wince with horror. Who was this sick individual and who was his hostage!? This question was on each of the officers' lips. Well, that among other things, like why did he have numerous trowels in his belt buckle? The sergeant gathers the officers up and begin planning. 'We're not calling for back-up because there're plenty of us here and we can't afford to distribute any more resources. It's up to us...and Jason.'

In Boss Michaels' office, Rob is on the computer trying to get it to work. He sighs. Shaun has a lawnmower up-side-down, attempting to salvage some key parts for his weapon collection. 'Are you on yet?' he asks Rob, who shakes his head. 'I think you smashed the internet when you were... smashing things,' Shaun scoffs, 'I know *exactly* what I hit. I hit his photos, his phone and the computer tower. I definitely didn't hit the router. There isn't even one here,' - 'You just said you hit the tower. The router is in the tower; he uses dial-up,' - 'You're kidding? Still!?' – 'You know how old-fashioned he is,' Rob says stubbornly. 'I'm so hungry, is there any food in this place?' asks Shaun. 'You can have a look in the fridge in the staff room but I think it's empty.' – 'No, I've just looked. Nowt. Ah, I'm really hungry man. Can we eat the coy carp? I brought some.' He reveals a small bag of coy carp, to Rob's astonishment. 'Why have you brought that? Do you realise how expensive they are? No, put them back,' – 'I think they'd go nicely in a sandwich, bit of tartare sauce.' He swings the bag backwards and forwards, taunting Rob. 'No, seriously, put them back. You remember how much I spilled last week, the stocks are fucked!' Shaun snorts 'Ah, come on, what's a few more gonna do?' Rob walks towards Shaun. 'Gis the fish,' he goes to grab it; Shaun plays with him like a little doggy. Rob gets a hand on it, Shaun moves backwards and trips over the lawnmower. The coy carp flies out of the bag and goes through a tiny gap in the barricaded window.

The officers, all of them in uniform now, line up outside a door to the stock room. Jason takes charge with the sergeant right behind him. Jason turns and addresses his squad 'OK, we'll breach and...' he turns to the sergeant 'clear?' the sergeant nods. Squabbling is heard above them, the sergeant signals silence. A coy carp flies out from above and lands right next to them. 'Here, these mean business,' whispers the fake hostage-taker. The sergeant looks at Jason; this is his moment. The sergeant nods and walks away, pulling his phone out. Jason steps back under the window, thinks long and hard and yells 'Why are you angry at the Mayans?'

Back in the office, Shaun and Rob stop fighting upon hearing Jason. They approach the window; Shaun quickly retaliates 'Because you're all fucking mental! Killing us all and that!' Rob gestures him to stop. 'Did you say 'you're all mental'?' replies Jason, now a lot calmer. 'Cause I saw you before, you took the real police into John Lewis and stole their clothes,' Rob watches Shaun as he speaks, nodding in agreement. 'Well, I assure you, we're not Mayans,' Jason says laconically. 'Aye, you would fucking say that, mate,' Rob tugs at Shaun's sleeve, 'maybe they're not Mayans,' he whispers. 'Eh? A minute ago you were asking where the army was, now you're on the bastard fence?' Shaun snaps back. 'Just let the hostage go and I promise you we'll sort something out.' Jason's voice carries through.

'Hostage?' Rob and Shaun both screech. 'Nice try!' shouts Shaun. 'Go and get the gnome.' He whispers to a dumbfounded Rob. 'What?' – 'I'm gonna prove to you that they're really Mayans. If they get one look at us, they'll not hesitate to blow us away. Get the gnome.' Rob excessively crawls to the other side of the room and retrieves the large gnome, which was hiding in the trolley. He returns to the window, in the same ridiculous crawling motion. Shaun takes his gas mask off and puts it on the gnome. He starts undressing completely. 'What are you doing!?' squeals Rob. 'This should be the last of your worries, I'm doing what has to be done.'

He dresses the gnome in his outfit and even puts the trowels in the gnome's new belt. 'So how are we going to do this?' asks Rob. 'I don't know, throw it? If they shoot it that means they're Mayans, if not, they're confused Mayans. We'll learn something about them either way.' Shaun snatches it, pulls the string from the window blinds and ties it on the gnome.

The gnome slowly descends from the window to the feet of the sergeant who has returned, *with Boss Michaels*. He looks down at the gnome, who stands smiling up at them, and then up at the window. Boss Michaels kicks it furiously into pieces. 'That's coming out of both of your wages,' he says deadpan. Back in the office, Rob squeals 'Oh shit. It's Boss Michaels!? Oh my god, *oh my god, oh my god*,' – 'Wait a minute, that means there aren't any Mayans! We're safe!' Shaun runs towards the window, arms-first. 'I'm not armed; I just want this to end!' The officers raise their weapons, Jason eases them. 'Alright, just come down to the...' he looks at his blueprints '...south door? This door. Come out this way.'

The sergeant escorts Boss Michaels away from the scene. 'Basically, when they come out, we'll do a thorough investigation as to what has happened and we'll take it from there,' explains the sergeant. 'Rob is one of my best employees, I can't say the same for Shaun but I'm just so surprised at Rob. What happened?' asks Boss Michaels. 'According to our sources, they thought the Mayans were coming.' They burst out laughing. 'The *Mayans?* That's the stupidest thing I've ever hea-' A poisonous blow-dart pierces Boss Michael's neck. A sea of Mayans burst onto the scene, stabbing the sergeant in the process. Their screams echo around the empty car park; the officers, caught off-guard, try and equip themselves but are quickly undone by the horde.

Shaun watches out of the window in horror. 'Oh my god, the Mayans. They actually came,' he cries. 'Yes, we did,' responds Rob. Shaun turns to Rob holding a hack saw. 'Rob? No... It can't be.' Rob hurls himself towards Shaun, 'then why is it?' The end.

'Haze'

Up to the point of writing this, I have been alive for 24 years, 328 days, 18 hours and 13 minutes. I have had some fairly big life experiences: dealing with loss, being in a long relationship, graduating from University, moving out and even going to Thorpe Park. Never in any of my conscious days have I had a life lesson which encapsulates the difficulties of life like this one. This moment, not only confirmed my understanding of *all this*, but helped me on the way to lower my expectations of what to aim for. This moment was when Haze came out.

Aye, it's a PS3 game. And it was shite. There was a considerable amount of hype, and those that know me know that I never really give in to hype, but I was really excited to play it. To me, it looked amazing. I watched so many gameplay videos of it; all my friends questioned it. 'Connor, I don't know what you're getting excited about, it looks fucking shite.' I was adamant that it looked crackin' but clearly I was a fool for thinking this. Everyone else was looking forward to the new Halo or Gears of War (Xbox shite) and I was sitting there creaming over Haze. Persona non grata.

Even Korn released a song for Haze called...Haze'. Aye, I know. *Korn* of all people. And it was shite. The music video showed the band performing the song, sandwiched in between clips of the game. And it was when I saw this video where I decided it looked shite. To this day, I still haven't played it and I refuse to. Forget about how curious I was and still am, about what it would be like to yield the controller and play Haze because I know I'll be let down. It would take me back to the hype I had for it. I'll remember my excitement and eagerness I had to play it. Then I'll be let down. Think about looking forward to something so much and then suddenly realizing 'ah, fuck. That's actually really shit and I will no way benefit from that experience.' In this instance, it's not about a game. It's about being let down. That's life.

Haze is life. The game represents life. It represents false hope. It represents decline. Haze is life and it's shite.

Area 51

it's on the floor

About ten years ago, my friend and I were walking down the arse-end of Bog Hall. Bog Hall is a little road, about two miles long, in between Lynemouth and Cresswell in Northumberland, a stone-throw away from the North Sea. I was wearing some new quarter length trousers, a poor choice as we were clarting around in the muddy ponds, throwing branches at trees and all that. I can't remember why we decided to venture that way; my house was the opposite direction.

As we were splodging through the mud to get to the nearest road; I thought it would be a good shortcut, it wasn't – we ended up fighting our way through a fucking swamp. Though we did come across a CD, lying face down in the Northumbrian ground. We picked it up and decided to keep it. There was no label on the front, it was one of those cheap rewriteable ones, but you could tell there was something on it because of the amount of scratches on the back – whether or not it would work was another question.

We brainstormed many different ideas of what could be on it – could it be some boring documents that a businessman no longer required? Or some banging tunes by MC SPIKE – 'on the mic 2nyt'? Or what if it was an EP by a band who don't exist anymore and threw their legacy out of a moving car so that one day, someone would find it and ask questions. That someone would listen to it and be amazed at the quality of the music. 'We have to recreate this music,' says that someone. He'll gathers his friends and get a band together, learn the music on the CD by ear, gig around with the material and sign a contract. Before he knows it, a CD on Cresswell beach has gained him and his band a massive following. Until one night, when that someone is at home with his supermodel lass, he hears a knock at the door. It's a long-haired man in a trench coat, out of breath and dripping from the rain he has fought through to get there. 'That was my CD,' he'll say in a gammy voice. Then the hairy man is like a mentor for that someone. I don't know how it ends, we didn't get that far. That'd be a good film, that.

After numerous possibilities, what it actually was, it was something we could have never dreamt up. We got back to mine, I got yarked off my mam and dad for getting my new pants hacky. 'Bollock is later, I've got a mystery to solve,' I said. We went up to my room and put the CD into the CD drive. And it was...

Gay porn. Nah, not really. It was weird at first, some sort of game. Like snakes and ladders but a lot harder. It was unusual but not disappointing – it only added more questions like 'what's gan on here!?' and 'who would put a shitty little game on a CD and throw it away?' Fuck knows, another question we asked ourselves was 'why are we still playing it?' – well that was simple: we couldn't let a game this low quality defeat us. We played and played and played until we won. It was hard though, harder than the last level of The Simpsons: Hit and Run. That was a game that I was never able to complete and that haunts me to the day of writing this. I wouldn't be beaten again. I grafted and grafted until I won. I couldn't believe it; my friend was asleep at this point. I don't know what kind of award I was expecting but what I got was...well, unexpected.

After I won, the screen turned green, not just the window that the game was in, my whole monitor was green. Maybe it was a System32 error or whatever the fuck. I went to restart my computer until words flashed along the bottom of the screen: 'Access Granted.' Weird. Is this a virus or something? Well, it couldn't have been because I had McAfee installed. Nothing can bypass that behemoth. The words faded, then the green went away. What was left was an image of a desk, filling the screen. It was like my point of view, sitting at the desk and I was surrounded by other blank monitors. I could look around with my mouse but none of my keys on my keyboard did anything. Some of the monitors I could see would flicker images of faces, mainly static though. The lights dimmed and a figure popped up in the middle of the table. He looked really important – he was wearing a *clean suit*. His lips were moving but I couldn't hear him; the CD started skipping; CD/DVD whatever the fuck it was. Apart from the skipping of the man and the flickering monitors, it was really good quality. There's no way there's only 150MB worth of space on this; this 'cut scene' was going on for ages. The figure then disappeared, followed by the monitors then the lights brightened up again.

I could move around the room now, using the WASD keys on the keyboard - like any other PC game. I had never been an avid PC gamer so I wasn't familiar with this game, if only the beginning hadn't messed up, I would've been able to follow the story a little bit better. I moved around the room but there were no doors, only large switches but I didn't know how to interact with them. There was another small monitor sat in the far side of the room. I walked over to it and pressed loads of random keys to access it. Finally, the L key on the keyboard did something – the monitor lights up and says 'Ellington, United Kingdom. 13/06/2006, 22:21:03, Participant: Connor Thompson, Eye Colour: Blue' – What the fuck? I look around my bedroom, nothing. What is going on? I notice my webcam is plugged in, but it's not even facing me – I unplugged it anyways. Fuck this. I decided to turn the whole thing off, it's too fucked up, this. How did it know? Why was my *eye colour* important? The off switch did nothing; I even unplugged the computer but it stayed on.

I ejected the CD and smashed the utter fuck out of it. Not having that hacker bullshit in my house. But guess what? It's *still* running. Zero sound coming from it, just the same POV of someone in the room. The graphics seemed lifelike – almost as if I was controlling a real person. The mouse was amazingly responsive to the game-thing; I could look around so easily. I looked around a bit more, walked towards more dead ends in the massive, conference room-type place. I went back to the computer; that was where I had the most luck. I pressed more keys. This time Alt+H made a list appear and I could select things on the list. I could choose five different options: 'submit new incident', 'review incident', 'submit new abduction', 'review abduction' and 'review species', I chose 'review abduction.'

The menu opened up a smaller menu with another five options: 'Roswell', 'Rendlesham Forest', 'George Adamski', 'Carlos Diaz' and 'Major Philip Corso'. I clicked back. What the fuck was this?

Back to the previous menu, I clicked on 'review species' - the room lit up even more. The switches around the room automatically switched on. The gaps next to the switches open up to reveal little compartments. Inside them were small cage-like boxes containing... aliens. Well that's what it says on the cages; they all have a label on the side of them 'ALIEN1' all the way to 'ALIEN8'. I couldn't actually see anything inside them from where I was. I slowly approached the one nearest to me and peaked inside. There was a tiny little... thing inside. Was this meant to be an alien? It didn't look like a generic one, not like the big headed Space Raider crisps, it looked like a cauliflower with teeth, no eyes until it opened its mouth to look around.

Its eyes met mine; I can't even move at this moment. It started speaking to me, not in any language I know of. He sounded like he was extremely flustered and warm. I look around to the other aliens, one looked like a stuffed bell pepper with Donald Trump's escaped barnet. And then it hit me, this wasn't a game, it was a portable network where one could access records instilled by the U.S. Government – this was Area 51; Area 51 wasn't a hidden location – it was a database!

I was on it every night for the next few months. Some of the shit I learned was fascinating and people talk about there being things hidden – take it from me, they have no idea; there are a *fuck tonne* of secrets. Unfortunately, those secrets are safe with me; The White House got in touch and said 'here, divint tell anyone like.' But what I will say is, Bog Hall is a nice place, especially if you big under the big tree next to the bike track. ;)

Socks

Yeah, I know. Socks. *Socks?* Aye, socks. I don't know what it is about them but I've got a sort of fucking rivalry with them. First of all, my feet are bogging. Fucking abominable, macabre pair of shits they are. I had ingrown toenails for absolutely ages – I actually remember being prescribed pills them, they were that bad. They didn't work though; the horrible infection just went away but have left me with these toes that are the size of tennis balls. That's all well and good, but the other side of my toe has really dry skin – my toes were once like mini-toasties.

The reason I don't like socks is because they just don't cut me a break. I can't keep a pair of socks in workable condition for very long at all without them getting holes in them. My socks have holes so big that the sock actually becomes nothing. The ones I have on right now are fine but only because I bought them about two weeks ago- they were a pack of five and these are the only ones left. That's five pairs equal to ten socks and I only have these two and about six individual socks left. I have lost a total of four socks in two weeks which may not seem like much but it is an extraordinary amount of socks to lose.

Something that annoys me about socks are the fashion necessity that one must always have a matching pair on at all times or don't bother. Why? They're designed to pamper my feet and protect them from pain, it's not like I can walk around in my bare feet, I haven't got Hobbit's feet. People call it common appearance rules to have matching pair but so what if I want to wear one sock with colourful patterns dancing around one foot and a standard black sock on the other foot. Why should I care about it? I'm wearing shoes anyways; you can't see my socks. Don't worry about my socks.

When I'm at home, people *can* see my socks, and this is the place I get criticised the most – I'm at home and I'm just trying to relax, leave me alone and don't worry about my socks.

I know what you're thinking – what the fuck have I just read? Why is this absolute dickhead going on about his socks in his own book? I'm afraid I don't have an answer for that. It's my book and this is a touchy subject for me and I wanted to address it. Please be careful when bringing this up with me, it's really hitting hard; I may need a minute before we progress to the next story.

Right, I'm ready now. I know there aren't that many 'stories' in this book but I promise the next one will be a longer, enjoyable tale and not just a pathetic, plaintive cry.

Sock count: 20

Fool's Gold

Graham worked at Daddy's Pawno for about twelve years – he didn't care much for the name of his inherited pawn shop; it wasn't his decision to keep the name, but instructed in his father's will to keep it the same name as *his* father gave it. Plus, the quirky name attracted business, so it wasn't the end of the world. Graham was the manager of the small shop, he had three employees – not a lot for running a shop but they were all very passionate about the business and understood that Graham couldn't afford to hire more staff.

Graham lives with his retired wife Anna, whose highlight of the day is when Graham comes home. They rarely see their kids who have their own families in different parts of the country – Anna's only source of company was sadly taken from her a few weeks ago when their beloved dog Benji was hit by a car. There were some lonely moments in their house since that regrettable day. Graham has offered to bring a new dog back but it's too soon and not the same.

Graham knew that he had to take her on holiday – something they hadn't done for close to ten years. The only problem was finance; Graham was barely making enough to live, let alone pay for a holiday. He knew in the back of his mind that Anna had a rather substantial pension but he couldn't ask her to blow it all on a week's holiday – that was to go towards their dream home and when Graham retires and gets *his* pension, they'd afford it. Graham wasn't ready to give up his shop anytime soon though, not until he left the shop in a profitable condition and found an heir to take over after him. It was a tricky business to run; how *do* pawn shops make profit? Well they basically rely on getting a better deal for goods that they buy for, Graham's father was a master at this – it came down to constantly keeping tabs on what is expensive at that time and what is selling well, he'd use websites like eBay and Amazon to see what a similar item is selling for used. Graham though, wasn't great at this. He would barely make a profit and end up selling everything for only a smidge more than he paid.

And that was part of the problem – business. Daddy's Pawno was a failing business, which was increasingly frustrating for Graham. It used to be so popular! People would sell everything there, televisions, laptops, necklaces, watches, everything. Even knackered stuff – Graham's dad knew how to salvage parts and make a profit from it; the same couldn't be said for Graham himself. His staff were getting fed up with Graham as well because they were regularly getting send home from their shifts and not making as much money. Graham hated doing this but his hands were tied.

Things started getting out of hand, Graham was beginning to tell his staff to not bother coming in for their shifts at all to try and save money. This eventually backfired when all of the staff decided to quit their jobs – not in a callous way; they emphasised sympathy for Graham but they needed a secure income. Graham had little to no options left – he would have to close the shop and try and get his early pension.

The final day of trade for the shop. One of his most loyal employees finished early after a long, empty morning. There's no point in anyone working today, Graham thought he may as well call a spade a spade and close the shop. He gets his coat and goes to leave but a shady man is stood at the door. He is tall and wears a top hat which, because of his heights, lightly brushes the ceiling. He is a tower. He holds out his hand towards Graham who stops in his tracks. 'This is worth everything,' he whispers. Graham, who was on his way out, goes back to the counter. 'Oh, we're about to close,' Graham says with reluctance. 'Big mistake,' - The man remains stood completely still, holding out small black bead-like objects. Graham stands on his tip toes to get a better look. 'What do you have there then? I've just took away the till,' The man finally moves closer, keeping his hand out. He approaches the counter and places them. 'Give me a tenner and we'll call it a day,' Graham observes them. 'What are they?' he asks. 'I can't say...but...it wouldn't be a bad idea in the sun...' He winks and then walks away dramatically.

He didn't even get his tenner, the weirdo. Graham looks closer at the junk, it basically looks like crushed up coal, but for some reason it looked valuable; it had a tint of a shine to it. He bagged it up and put it in his pocket. Graham never really got any strange folk in his shop, not that Graham judged anyone, all that mattered was profit and there was none there. He drove home in an awful mood. There goes Anna's holiday that he had been relentlessly planning for years. He stops the car for a cry then continues.

He gets home and Anna lies asleep on the couch, still with her gardening gloves on. Graham kisses her head softly and goes to the garden to see what beautiful flower Anna has in bloom.

There were a few tulip seeds planted next to Benji. As he falls into a loving trance, next door's dog bellows screechy, awful barks – the dog was tiny but not cute and it spoiled Graham's moment with *his* dog who was with them no longer. It was clear that Anna wanted to make a shrine for Benji. He ignored the yapping from Scrappy fucking Doo and smiles at the grave pleasantly with his hands in his pockets, he feels the crushed up charcoal shite in his pocket, his smile fades and he angrily launches it in the garden. 'What are you doing?' Anna squeals, up and out of the couch in a moment. 'Sorry, Anna, just had a hard day,' He retorts. He goes into the garden and tries to pick up everything, leaving a couple of crumbs behind.

It chucked it down through the night, Graham watched the rain from his bed – people like to fall asleep to the rain, not Graham. Especially with defeat looming over him. All in all, he got around two hours sleep; he was woken up by next door's little dog barking insufferably under the fence. He traipses downstairs to put the kettle on. He yawns and looks out the window to see the tulips have fully blossomed. Graham shouts for Anna, 'How have they grown that quickly?' he shouts up the stairs. They weren't even normal sized tulips; they were like the biggest tulips ever. Gigantulips. Another strange thing was that there were no puddles on the grass, could the tulips have drunk *all* of that water? Impossible! There was also a small bulb over where Benji had been buried, next door's dog kept barking. Graham shushes the dog as he picks some tulips and lays them on Anna's pillow. 'Penny, inside. Now!' bellows the neighbour.

Graham looks around town for jobs, its futile but he couldn't sit around and do nothing all day. He could work in a bar – nah, too old. He could clean some toilets – nah, Graham was a germophobe. Forget it. He would have to just go back home and read the paper and complain about black people like all the other old people. It wasn't in his nature to do nothing, he thought he would build a shed when he retires but he didn't feel that he chose the retirement which is why it feels like a defeat.

He returns home with some plywood and a hammer, may as well get started. He begins brainstorming what he could put in the shed. Could put a fridge there for some home brew or something. It could be a place where he could chill out; finally, somewhere to put his dart board! He gets off the bus and sees numerous cars outside his next door neighbour's house. A woman scrambles towards Graham. 'Have you seen Penny!?' she pleads. Graham shakes his head, hardly even noticing her losing her little shite of a dog. He wasn't a cold person but that dog was a nightmare. The reason he hardly noticed her was his attention was on his own house. Or rather, behind his house – his garden. He could see a huge bulb-like thing from the other side of his house. He darted to the garden to see it was the same bulb over Benji. There was a stem that went into the earth and went into a massive egg-shaped plant thing. How was such a thin stem holding up something so heavy? Graham thought the cars were for the neighbour's dog, but he noticed dozens of people standing in his garden videoing it. 'Who are you people? Get out of my garden!' He yelled. Anna waved him to stop. 'What!?' he yells back, she rushes over and whispers in his ear 'I've been charging a couple of quid a head,' Graham winces in disbelief. This is way too much to take in, first of all his seemingly good natured wife is now a haggler, next door's little rat was missing and there's a massive, pulsating testicle in his back garden. Graham needed a shot and Graham doesn't even drink.

Weeks pass and the bulb is now the size of an airplane, not the shape of course but the size was indeed to scale; it was humongous. The tulips were dead though; the garden was flooded with huge dead flowers as there wasn't enough water in the English weather (if you can believe that) to keep them alive. Then what, I hear you ask, was keeping the bulb alive? That question was what attracted worldwide press and tourists to see the phenomenon. The neighbours would attempt to sabotage the press to get the word out about their still-missing dog. It didn't work though – they were fascinated with the bulb and so was Graham. Documentaries were being made about it, which led interest to Graham and his story about the strange man who gave him the crumbled up object.

Graham became a celebrity because of the bulb. He appeared in numerous magazines where he flaunted his story; it got him plenty of money, so why wouldn't he? The dream holiday was still on his mind, regardless of everything that was going on. He'd get stopped in the street from people asking to come around and see the Big Bulb. He had been to buy a fan as his bedroom was stuffy; they couldn't get their window open because the sodding thing! 'Of course you can come,' he beamed.

He trots them back to his house, getting bombarded with press as usual – 'off the grass, Anne's just planted them!' he politely asks, pointing at the soil. He makes his way to the garden, spotting many sheets with missing dog posters scattered across his fence. He leads his followers to his garden where the bulb looks noticeably smaller. 'Oh, it looks much bigger on the tele,' one of them says. 'No, it's usually massive!' Graham urgently steps inside his house to find Anna. 'What's happened to my bulb? It's much smaller,' he says with dismay. 'I don't know, it was fine this morning but it's just slowly shrinking,' she says pressing a cup of tea to her lips. She didn't seem bothered.

Graham returns to the garden where many of the people he had brought have scattered out. 'Where are you going? I haven't even charged you yet!' he nervously laughs, 'well, it's not that good is it?' one man said. Graham looked back at it, it was still getting smaller, almost as if it was a balloon with the microscopic hole letting the air out. Everyone left, Graham walked towards the bulb which was making a very quiet growl, almost like a pathetic plea for help. But it was a plant, how was it making a sound? The bulb getting smaller more and more quickly now and the noises getting even more faded. Graham looks at it up and down, seeing Benji's grave and... hold on. Could it be? That this plant, this *thing*, has miraculously brought Benji back to life? Well, why not? The tulips' size was thought impossible since it happened, why not this? The yelp happened again and it sounded just like him. Graham rushes to his half-built shed and gets the hammer, he starts hacking at the bulb – 'I'm coming Benji!' he screams. He hacks and hacks and hacks – the bulb is no more.

He throws aside bits of stem, roots and scales from it and there, laying underneath it all was a dog. But it wasn't Benji, it was the next door neighbour's dog. Dead.

Sex Casm

Lpul.zsaq21`,`` `o zs zsssssssssssssssssssssssssssssslnl sps\   FFFF4 V6 D
BVC VV V
Y T B TM NM | Qa|AS5DFAAASEEEER HHUGHUMKMLHJ

MNKJIJHJUGNM RE21ZX M   ,8M MI EA   3WDCASDXZO QARASDXZO
NNQARERFDDDRRRRRRRRRRRRRRRRRRRRRRRRRRRRRRRRRRRRRRRRRRRRRRRRRRR
RRRRRRRRRRRRRRRRA|WS\AF AZ\5,SD5RESEEEEEEEEEEEEEEEEEEEEEEEEDZ
RRRRRRRRRRRRRRRRRRRRRRRRRRRRRRRRRRRRRRRRRRRRRRRRRRRRRRRRRRRRRR
RRRRRRRRRRRRRRRRRRRRXLL..
................RD\2WASEXCASMGFWQ   \ZBN M

BY JOEL, 8 MONTHS

Printed in the United States
By Bookmasters